33 REVOLUTIONS

Canek Sánchez Guevara

33 Revolutions

*Translated from the Spanish
by Howard Curtis*

Europa
editions

Europa Editions
214 West 29th Street
New York, N.Y. 10001
www.europaeditions.com
info@europaeditions.com

Translation by Howard Curtis
Original title: *33 revoluciones*
Translation copyright © 2016 by Europa Editions

Library of Congress Cataloging in Publication Data is available
ISBN 978-1-60945-348-0

Sánchez Guevara, Canek
33 Revolutions

Book design by Emanuele Ragnisco
www.mekkanografici.com

Prepress by Grafica Punto Print – Rome

Printed in the USA

33 REVOLUTIONS

Beyond the window, everything moves: paper trees, toy cars, stick houses, straw dogs. Foam spreads through the streets like a stain, leaving water, seaweed, and broken things in its wake, until the next wave, when everything will start all over again. The tide uproots what the wind is unable to demolish. The building withstands the battering. Inside, the corridors seem full of frightened faces and people reciting instructions and obvious truths ("We have to keep calm, comrades: nothing is eternal"). Everyone talks at the same time (twenty scratched records playing at the same time): they all say the same thing in different words, like when they're standing in line or at a meeting—an obsession with talking: twelve million scratched records blathering on without stopping. The whole country is a scratched record (everything repeats itself: every day is a repetition of the day before, every week, month, year; and from repetition to repetition, the sound deteriorates until all that is left is a vague, unrecognizable recollection of the original recording—the music disappears, to be replaced by an incomprehensible, gravelly murmur). A transformer explodes in the distance and the city is plunged into darkness. The building is a black hole in the middle of this universe that insists on loudly breaking down. Nothing works, but it's all the same. It's always the same. Like a scratched record, always repeating itself . . .

The wind comes in through the cracks, the pipes hiss, the building is a multifamily organ. Nothing can compare with the music of the cyclone; it's unique, unmistakable, exquisite. In the small apartment, the walls, painted a nondescript color, with no decorations or images, combine with the sparse furniture, the wooden TV set, the Russian record player, the old radio, the camera hanging from a nail. The telephone off the hook, books on the floor. Water seeps in through the windows, soaks the walls, forms pools on the floor. Mud. Grime and more grime. A grimy scratched record. Millions of grimy scratched records. The whole of life is a grimy scratched record. Repetition after repetition of the scratched record of time and grime.

In the kitchen, two cans of condensed

milk, one of meat stew, a bag of cookies. On the side, an egg, a piece of bread, a bottle of rum. Some food past its expiration date, with mold on it. The whisk on a corner of the little table; the frying pan on the stove (grease on the wall); and the refrigerator from the Fifties, empty and switched off, with the door open. The bed is in the middle of the bedroom. The bathroom is tiny, dark, without water. The shower is hardly ever used: the bucket and the jug have replaced it. The tube of toothpaste, the deodorant, the razor. The broken mirror paints a scar on his reflection.

He goes out onto the balcony and is hit by a gust of wind. Anonymous in the immensity of the storm, abandoned to his fate, replaying the scratched record of life and death, he lights a cigarette and looks out at that apocalyptic postcard. Time and again, like a scratched record, he wonders why everything appears unchangeable even though each mutation brings upheavals. The building withstands, yes, but everything else sinks into the seaweed and the dead things left by the tide. Finally, he smiles: with the passing of the days, the sea will recover from its tropical illness and the repetitive cycle of routine will return, like a scratched record, to meet normality.

The scratched record of work. The office, the photograph of the leader, the metal desk, the chair that gives him hemorrhoids, the fat old typewriter, the ballpoint pen to one side, the yellowing papers, the rubber stamps, the telephone. The manager appears. He flaps his double chin, smooths down his white shirt, and clears his throat before speaking. His voice is like a flute when he receives orders and a trombone when he gives them. Like now. The manager walks out of the office, leaving behind him the echo of a slamming door. At last, he is alone in his office, blacker, skinnier, and more nervous than usual. Slightly more subordinate too.

The telephone rings, and the skinny, nervous black man replies without much conviction. All he can hear through the wires is noise—far away, like a scratched record—and he hangs up. He goes to the window and lights a cigarette. Life stops in front of his eyes, and doesn't surprise him at all. When it comes down to it, he thinks, it's always been like this, stasis disguised as dynamis. He glances at his self-winding Soviet watch: Ten in the morning, and already he can't stand his job. Of course, he's never liked it, but now he's truly sick of it (and immediately, in parenthesis, he wonders when this started). Evening after evening he goes back to his solitary apartment, and morning after morning he leaves it to its solitude. The neighbors are a bunch of scratched records, devoid of interest. As for the committee, you just have to obey silently, come out with a few *Vivas!*, and everybody's happy.

In reality, nobody cares about anybody else.

Lunchtime. The dining room is filled to the brim with technicians and bureaucrats, and the line is so long, it's like there's a movie premiere happening. The food is as cheap as it is limited, but it's better than nothing and everybody's grateful for it. "What are they giving us today?" those waiting ask those coming out. "Same as yesterday," they reply apathetically. When at last it's his turn, he looks lazily at the military tray: the circle of vegetable stew, the square of rice, the rectangle of sweet potato, the glass in its ring, and the knife, fork, and spoon in their groove. He eats it all in ten minutes and goes out to look for cigarettes. What little shade there is from the noonday sun is unable to allay the heat, let alone the humidity of this jungle of decaying structures and centuries-old beauty. The sea can be glimpsed in the distance, but today its breeze is pure absence. He sends a moan up into the sky and stops outside the store on the corner: A handwritten sign says, "No cigars or coffee."

Like a scratched record, he moans once again.

Duty and desire. Angrily, he bangs out his dilemma on the typewriter until the paper is perforated with periods and commas. His desire is to be alone in this office, in this city, in this country, and never to be disturbed. Monotony is expressed in a thousand ways and acquires various signs. Work, radio, news bulletins, meals, free time: I live in a scratched record, he thinks, and every day it gets a bit more scratched. Repetition puts you to sleep, and that sleepiness is also repeated; sometimes the needle jumps, a crackling is heard, the rhythm changes, then it sticks again. It always sticks again.

He hears loud footsteps beyond the door, and he knows who they belong to. Where's the report? I'll have it ready in a while, he replies. The manager glares at him, veins in his nose, a surly look in his eyes, the son of a bitch. The manager reprimands him without a single hair falling out of place (a lot of gel, a lot of cologne, a lot of talcum on the neck, he thinks). He feels like telling him to go fuck himself, and fuck his mother, and while he's about it, go fuck his whole life, but all he can do is move his head from side to side with no rhythm or meaning, unable to understand why he's being reprimanded and for what.

"Listen to me!" the master roars. "Are you listening to me?"

The day's work is over. Eight hours of
checking and stamping papers, signing
memos, writing reports, making copies,
putting up with the manager, and not much
more. Eight hours as interminable as summer or solitude. Eight hours devoted to
nothing. But today is payday, and that
seems to give meaning to the everyday
nihilism, the farce of making a contribu-
tion, the madness of giving service.

He sniffs the envelope of rough yellow
paper with his name handwritten on it and
counts those colored bills whose value, as
he well knows, is as relative as our reality.
He doesn't want to go home. He thinks
he'd rather go get an ice cream; he walks
unhurriedly, watching the scratched
records pass with their end-of-month
smiles, full of wage-earner's pride. There's

no silence in the city: Everyone talks at the same time, more than usual, echoing the buzzing of bumblebees—and the women, the buzzing of the queen bee. All the women think they're queens here. At last he gets to the ice cream parlor, and the length of the line destroys his craving. He walks on past (should he go into the movie theater? Forget it). He turns onto San Lázaro, plunges down a side street, and runs aground in a corner bar, dark and perfumed with men's urine: a long bar counter, dirty tables, cheap rum: nothing more. Nobody smiles, nobody greets him. Everyone minding his own business.

In a corner, four guys are playing dominoes, as they do every day of the year and every year of time. There's never any variation in the parade of white pieces, black dots, double nines, cries, curses. Next to each player, the eternal glass of rum; in the middle, the ashtray full of cigarette butts. This, he thinks, is the scratched record of national culture. In another corner, a taciturn woman, dressed in synthetic polychrome clothes, talks to herself as she leafs through yesterday's newspaper. Four pages, all the same, with the same tone, the same glibness, the same old song, the words, the anger.

The woman grumbles.

He sits down at the bar, orders a rum, lights a cigarette, and rambles to himself; the universe is a scratched record with no relativity or quanta, full of grooves down which this life of cosmic dust, industrial grease, and common tar passes, he thinks. He takes a swig of his drink, makes a noise with his throat, and tilts his head, nauseated and grateful.

Rum is the hope of the people, he thinks.

The moon is full when he comes out of the bar, but its light barely filters between the buildings. He walks, avoiding narrow alleys and dark corners. On the avenue, there's a concert; the crowd is like a tide, moving to the rhythm of congas and trumpets, and he melts into it. He dances alone in the midst of a commotion that isolates him as it surrounds him, and he wonders what it means to belong, to be united. Is the communion of other people's bodies merely the alienation of the ordinary? In any case, he thinks, here again is the scratched record of fortuitous encounters or failed encounters, anonymous and indifferent (without forethought or calculation: pure nocturnality), on this avenue where sensuality, equality, and the urge for human solidarity converge. The only thing that works here, he thinks, is partying, promiscuity, phallocentrism, an obsession with sex (erotic materialism). The rest is speechmaking to confuse the masses. Sex is the beginning and the end: History as one big fuckfest, he thinks.

And there, amid the music, the sweaty bodies, and the cans of beer, he remembers his ex-wife, always sick with frigidity. The marriage didn't last long: a scratched record of arguments and grievances whose gradual deterioration ended in rigor mortis. Her asexuality led him to impotence, blackened his mood, poisoned his already limited optimism. At first, he thought it was reserve, shyness, and that time and trust would put an end to these blemishes. But it was something deeper. Far from improving, the situation got worse. They spent weeks with no more intimacy than you get in a meal you eat by yourself, until sex disappeared entirely from their lives (along with caresses, smiles, and words). He made up his mind to leave her after a disturbing dream: fed up with her, and taking advantage of her sleep, he slashed her to death with a machete as she lay in bed, spattering the walls of the room. He woke with a start, realized that he had ejaculated, and the following morning, very early, left home and never went back—months, maybe years later, they negotiated a divorce, when the resentments and grievances had faded away.

Still dancing, he reaches the seawall, buys a bottle of diluted rum, sits down facing the waves, and compares their movement with the movement on the wall, which is full of couples feeling each other up, groups causing a ruckus, and loners like me, he thinks: Watching time pass is the people's favorite pastime. Not wasting it, which would imply that they had it to waste. The years remain, he thinks: Time always passes . . .

He looks down at the sea again and drinks straight from the bottle. Behind him, the dirty, beautiful, broken city; in front of him, the abyss that suggests defeat. It isn't even a dilemma, let alone a contradiction, but the certainty that it's this abyss, this isolation, that defines and conditions us. We win by isolating ourselves, and in isolating ourselves we are defeated, he thinks. The wall is the sea, the screen that protects us and locks us in. There are no borders; those waters are a bulwark and a stockade, a trench and a moat, a barricade and a fence. We resist through isolation. We survive through repetition.

Gradually, the seawall empties. It's nearly dawn and he thinks about going home. He proceeds along an avenue without cars or people, with few trees, and buildings that seem to grow straight up from the curb. Behind him, he hears the rumble of a bus, and he sets off at a run for the next stop. He only has two hundred yards to go when the wail of a patrol car stops him. The cops get out, look him up and down, focus on the bottle, and demand his papers.

"Identity card!"

"Comrades," he replies, "I'm going to miss the bus."

"Later," they reply. "First the card."

He hands over the identity card, and the other one too. The cops smile. They check the information. They apologize for their procedure.

"Sorry, comrade. You know how it is. A black man running in the dark is always suspicious . . . "

The alcohol wears off, the lights of the bus blink in the distance, and his blackness turns pale with rage. He remembers the day they gave him the card (not the identity one, the other one): The dumb smile with twinkles of pride, the unique sensation of being part of a new, vigorous, redemptive future. But tomorrow is built on the grave-yard of yesterday with the workforce of today. Only later would he realize that the image of the future isn't, cannot be, the future itself.

A steady stream of expletives keeps him going until he gets to his building. He sighs when he sees the elevator stuck on the first floor (the scratched record of things that never work) and apathetically climbs the seven floors. In his apartment, solitude greets him in all her nakedness and invites him to lie down beside her. Arrogantly, he throws himself onto the couch alone and puts on an old record that's scratched in the middle and stutters like wayward percussion. He switches off the record player and goes out onto the balcony to smoke, facing the darkness that is the sea.

The dawn blurs. The police have snatched away his dream and something he wouldn't call pride, let alone dignity, but which is doubtless important. He's upset because they let him know (reminded me? he wonders with a smile) that he's a lousy nigger. On the balcony, in his shorts, bare-chested, he thinks there isn't one iota of greatness in any of this, and he makes a gesture that tries to take in the whole city, maybe the whole country. But he's always been immersed in the legend, in all the organizations, speeches, marches, delegations, and commitments. Always with his head held high.

It was during his last years of university that he started to change, even though he can't pinpoint the exact moment or the exact situation, already diffused by time, in which such a thing happened, nor what this change actually consisted of.

The needle jumped, he thinks.

Father was what in sociological terms might be called an ignorant peasant; Mother, on the other hand, was a delightful young lady from the city who had been brought up to marry well and not much more—elementary English, basic piano, international cooking: all that's required to get along in society. It isn't hard to understand that in the revolutionary maelstrom a union like that could occur: The country was being rapidly transformed and some barriers fell ostentatiously, fostering relationships that would once have been impossible or unthinkable. Father joined the revolutionaries months before their triumphal entry, and Mother sold bonds for the 26th of July Movement in her smart new car. They met—or rather, bumped into each other—at one of those huge meetings where anger and fervor fused, and further encounters in various associations and assemblies ended up giving rise to an awareness that they were equal, that they had the same dreams, were part of a project that included them and made demands on them equally. Later, Father would work in agrarian reform and Mother in light industry.

There were hardly any books in the house—just the doctrinal works, more out of correctness than to be read—and as for music, the radio was always enough. He was a diligent but not outstanding pupil. He had little interest in the arts or in mathematics, nor was he very good at science. But he always scored highly for conduct, and was unstinting in his participation in patriotic activities, however boring they might be. His studies were technical—including some engineering—almost devoid of cultural, sporting, or work-related interests: The nation comes first, he would always say with conviction. He put his heart and soul into everything and always got the top grades. He was head of his class, of his school, and of various departments and federations, and there are those who remember him informing on comrades who lacked political and ideological commitment. In short, he was a model student: not brilliant but certainly committed. Until one day he started reading; first timidly, almost fearfully—as if it was something forbidden—and then addictively: sprawled on the couch, with cookies in one hand and the book in the other.

"Do something!" Father would shout, unable to comprehend, but Mother, always Mother, would tell her husband that he shouldn't get upset, that maybe the boy would become an intellectual.

"An intellectual?" Father would bellow, convinced that artists (and similar people) are a disaster for the country. And he was right, decades earlier he had followed with interest the debates with those so-called intellectuals who seemed more like agents of the enemy—deviationists!—people who suffered from the original sin: lack of revolutionary spirit. "And you're not going to

be like them! No way!" (Behind him,
Mother would be making signs that meant:
Don't mind him, son: Don't mind him at
all).

He read a lot—quite unaware, in no particular order and with no particular inten-
tion—and continued with his studies
because he had discovered a private universe much vaster than the one around him.
As it turned out, that universe highlighted
the narrowness of everyday life and made
him dream of unknown, missing expanses.
That was when everything started to seem
like a scratched record.

The needle gets stuck in a groove and the tropical avenue seems full of Urals, Volgas, Moskviches, and Polskis. Inside, the air conditioning and the diplomat store full of nice things. Outside, the scalding tar of the street, the nonexistent breeze, and the thirst; inside, cold beer, consumer goods, and food; outside, the hunger and the silence. Two worlds in one, two dimensions, two universes: Two nations and two deaths, he thinks: The needle crackles, jumps, and falls here, where nothing is permitted but everything is decided and done.

"What blockade?" he asks himself, gazing at the shelves full of foreign products at prices incompatible with the national economy, and he's amazed, not by what there is, but by what there isn't outside this consumerist enclave.

He has a slight hangover and with slow movements, close to cramps, he reaches out his arm and grabs a cold Coke: He opens it there and then, whistling "The March of the Fighting People," and devotes himself to it with almost aesthetic—even ideological—delight, smiling like a child doing something wrong when nobody's looking.

He doesn't go to the diplomat store alone, but with the Russian woman from the ninth floor, the one who's in charge of the black market in the building. She's the one with the passport, the one who legally has foreign currency and the right to buy. When they come out, they part affectionately (he pays her a commission to get him in): Father didn't get to see this, he thinks. He died years ago, when it was discovered that in the agricultural concern that he ran there was a big shortfall, and they blamed him.

"Misappropriation of funds!" was the expression used during the trial, and he, always so pure, kept angrily, indignantly proclaiming his innocence:

"For fuck's sake, nobody calls me a thief!" he shouted at the top of his lungs, red in the face, until his heart burst.

"Massive heart attack," said the doctor.

The night of the funeral, getting drunk with his friends, it struck him that his father had died of innocence (and he said, by way of farewell, showing his white teeth in a sad, inebriated smile, that he had been pigheaded but honest, ignorant but idealistic). Mother, after a few months of grief—wandering from home to work and from work to home—decided to process her Spanish citizenship (on her father's side) and left for Madrid: She is the one who sends him a bit of money and a few books every now and then.

He doesn't like to walk down the street with shopping bags, that's why he puts everything in his backpack. Actually, he hasn't bought much: a bit of meat, rice, eggs, oil, bread, two or three beers, a bottle of rum, cigarettes, toothpaste, deodorant, shampoo: the basics (don't even mention the ration book): He eats little and his taste is limited; besides, he has lunch at work: What more can I ask for in this world? he asks himself sarcastically. On the outside, he seems a normal guy, shabbily dressed, with an ordinary face and eyes that say nothing: One more scratched record, he murmurs to himself.

And on the inside?

He asks himself lots of questions. He's afraid he'll discover that in reality he's a long-suffering narcissist enchanted with his own existential misery: Like a damned *poète maudit*, he thinks (he looks at the people at the bus stop, focuses on their absent looks, so similar to his, and starts walking along Fifth, downcast and smiling).

Like one more . . .

At times in his youth he thought about changing course, giving up engineering and switching to philosophy and letters, or history, or even social science, but he constantly put his father's judgements and values before his own plans. When his father was alive, he was afraid he would kill him with fright, and once he was dead he decided to respect his wishes: But that was his fault, not Father's. On the other hand, he's never been able to write—he knows he's incapable of putting together a single sentence: he considers himself simply a reasonable, inquiring reader, and makes no other claims. His work at the ministry is boring but encourages reading: he covers the books with newspaper and if anyone in the office asks what he's reading, he invariably replies: Agatha Christie (although it's actually Kundera).

But the most important discovery of the past few years has been music—before, he didn't have music; he listened to what his friends listened to (if he was with timba fans, timba; with trova fans, trova; with jazz fans, jazz; with rock fans, rock . . . and so on, without dwelling on anything in particular). Without any preferences. He found no meaning in that explosion of sounds: Sometimes he danced, more out of an instinct to be sociable or as part of the mating ritual than out of true, autonomous pleasure. Music, in short, meant nothing to him.

It happened after he and his wife separated: He decided to go to the theater to listen to the symphony. There was no curiosity in that decision (or maybe only a little), rather, the other options struck him as worse—baseball at the stadium, a comedy at the movie theater, TV with its two channels: No, thanks. The program included pieces by Roldán and Brouwer. For the first time he was able to dream while music played. Those sounds—those twisted chords—made him jump for joy, with an inexplicable happiness, closer to neurosis than spiritual calm. For weeks he lived with that sensation in his body; suddenly he knew that he had encountered the music he'd been missing. Over time, he's managed to put together a modest but well-organized collection of avant-garde, serial, aleatoric, mathematical, modernist, and minimalist music, and every now and again he wonders what he's done to deserve this—to have tastes so alien to the tropics and yet live here . . .

He pours himself a beer, switches on the TV with the volume very low—voices in the background: a bit of company—and puts on a Varèse cassette at full volume. He goes back to the kitchen and fries himself a steak; he gobbles it down on a piece of bread with oil and garlic, sitting at the little table. He synchronizes the end of the sandwich with the last note of the recording. He grabs a book and tries to concentrate, all the while fighting against the heat. He needs company: After the separation he decided that never again would he have a woman in his home, at least for more than one night. He leads a healthy sex life with himself, and he only mates when necessary—if he wants to smoke and talk while looking up at the ceiling—not every time he needs to ejaculate: He's convinced it's healthier this way. He feels particularly attracted to women over forty, but they have to be married or recently divorced. He can't stand spinsters: Too maternal, he thinks.

It was around the end of his matrimonial crisis (at the age of twenty-five) that he started to develop a taste for older women; at first out of curiosity—morbid curiosity?—then out of conviction. Everything started with a neighbor, the wife of a soldier who spent more time in his unit than at home. They met while on guard duty for the committee, and they talked and talked for hours about things as intimate as delays in meat distribution or the limited variety of food available in the market. Somehow they ended up involved in a secret relationship in a building full of gossips (actually, the threat of gossip was the least risky part of the affair: The one danger was the husband, a man who—he thinks—wouldn't hesitate to put a bullet in his balls).

He gets up slowly and goes up to the ninth floor in search of the Russian woman. She opens the door and leans back against the doorframe, as if she had guessed he was coming. The night passes slowly—they know each other, they've learned to delight in prolonged, stuttering spasms—and toward the end, he snorts loudly. He smokes, lying in the dark against the woman's naked back—powerful buttocks that wear out sheets and dreams—and he thinks that metaphors are unnecessary at this moment in which the smoke drifts up to the ceiling, slithering amid the aromas of sweat, sex, and tropicalism.

She sleeps and he devotes himself to sniffing her body (the smell of her hairy underarms burns his nostrils and jangles his neurons). Without putting pressure on her, he makes her turn—her tits point up at the ceiling; he buries his nose in her pubis, filling his lungs with the unmistakable acidity of that lush blond cunt, full of socialist realism. She smiles in her sleep—she murmurs something in Russian (she's back in the steppes)—and he lies down to smoke once again, letting himself be borne along by the scratched record of pleasure and tiredness.

15

His peace is broken by a shower of night-sticks and boots. He tries to wake, shaky, eyes imploring, naked, he wonders what he's done, what he's said, and he yells at the top of his lungs. His body is burning and he feels every muscle atrophied by fear. He's flung down the stairs, and as he goes down he bumps on a surface that's not very pleasant to the touch. He's surrounded by insults, anger, madness. More kicks, many more. Now he weeps. He doesn't want to, but he can't help it. His teeth. His teeth hurt. Downstairs, they bundle him into a new Mercedes that jolts in time to the blows.

Villa Marista. They drag him to an interrogation room. A shaky doctor certifies that there's no serious damage to this weary, skinny individual who's trembling as much as he is. Two officers come in and threateningly demand that he tell them everything. One of them hits him full in the face; the other insults his mother, calls him a fag, and gives him a thump in the sternum.

"Talk, for fuck's sake!" they both roar simultaneously.

16

They lock him in a cell with two unsavory-looking characters. He crouches in a corner, sniffles, and tries to come to terms with the pain. He looks up; the prisoners are watching him and smiling.

"Did you talk?" one of them asks.

"Talk about what?"

He's on the verge of despair. He doesn't understand why he's here, and has no idea how to get out. Everything is fear at that moment. A fear that eats away at him, humiliates him more than the blows, the shouts, the insults. He doesn't care whether or not there are witnesses to his panic, his paralysis: I'm the witness, he thinks, judging himself harshly now that he can finally breathe a little more easily. The cell stinks. It's cramped and gray and there are stains on the wall that look like dried blood.

There's a small window, just enough to bring in a little air; it's almost at the level of the ceiling, unreachable for a man of medium height.

He lies down on a concrete cot, as cold and hard as the cemetery. He can't close his eyes. He's afraid to do so. A long series of distorted images unfurls on the ceiling, reminding him of *A Clockwork Orange*. Three short but well-built guards shove him out and force him to walk along endless corridors. They come to a dark room lit by a single dim bulb. In it, a high-ranking officer (it's unmistakable) is waiting for him; they sit him down on a chair and before he can open his mouth a thick volume of *Das Kapital* crashes into his left parietal.

"Talk!" the man with the stripes murmurs from the semidarkness.

"About what?"

"You know."

"I don't know anything. I don't understand . . . "

The guards look at each other, one murmurs something about a son of a bitch, and the other lets fly with the second volume, this time full in the face and with the spine. Blood spurts from his nose (nasal septum shattered). Unbearable pain, tears that burst against his tightly closed eyelids, real howls.

Then he wakes up, soaked in sweat, next to the Russian woman, who at that moment grunts something untranslatable.

He dresses quickly.

He escapes to reality . . .

17

Eight A.M. The heat and humidity are
already unbearable (the atmosphere sur-
passes any instrument of measurement:
Something indescribable hovers in the air).
The bus advances toward the slaughter-
house of the everyday (people hanging from
doors and windows, men rubbing up
against women in the interior—the morning
hard-on) and at last stops at the intersection
of two avenues trapped in time. Already
tired, he walks to work with the certainty of
futility—the discontent, the atrophy, the
silence of everyday life. The office awaits
him like last week: There are no surprises or
changes or novelties. Once the epic is
exhausted, all that remains is the boredom,
the absenteeism, the indifference (con-
sciousness is unpredictable; without feed-
back, it scratches, the needle jumps, and it

becomes incomprehensible, inscrutable, impossible to grasp). Everything lacks definition; dirt erases the most basic forms (theft is a legitimate practice): Blackmail unites, decline disguises itself as progress, and even so the record keeps turning (the needle sticks, jumps, and goes backwards): Confusion is the one certainty.

He knows: Today nothing will go well. On days like this, life seems to him a vain literary exercise, an experimental poem, a treatise on the pointless and the unnecessary, and he walks slowly, his eyes glued to the ground, wishing he could fall onto the curb and die crushed by habit. He lights a cigarette, blows out the smoke, and looks behind him (beyond time). He thinks that, after all, reality is a strange place, at least here. Determinedly, he turns and walks in the opposite direction. He gets in a battered old heap that stinks of kerosene, squashed between six strangers.

Through the windshield he sees the scratched world pass by, like a record in which everything happens (the city, white

with so much light, the people on the stair-
cases, in doorways, and on balconies staring
into space; people standing in line, break-
downs). The driver keeps complaining: the
gasoline, the tires, the spare parts (the
grammar of movement, words in perpetual
motion). The Capitolio: itinerant photographers, tourists, teenage tearaways in trendy
clothes, police officers with their eyes
peeled, adults engaged in the unequivocal
dialectic of idleness . . .

He walks. He listens to conversations:

"Down with the union!" someone cries.

"Everything's for sale here, man."

"Fuck off!" another replies.

"Fuck you! You're a fucking faggot, you
know that?"

"Scram, pal," the crowd is getting
worked up (indignation): the ethics of fists
and guns.

"Just get the hell out of here, things are
turning ugly . . . "

Cops in a patrol car. He gets to the stop
and asks to be dropped at the end of the
waiting line. People on all sides—scratched

records that nobody listens to (statistics for a speech or a balance sheet): But they aren't the ones who'll be left, he thinks: I'm the one who'll be left.

Santa María, burning hot sand, scratched records in tangas or Bermuda shorts. He watches a group of young people who look out to sea with a mixture of fatalism and anxiety (the distance seems so distant from here): Schizophrenia is normal in this scratched record—side A, side B—a mix that leads nowhere, bipolar phenomenology. He walks barefoot with the bottoms of the pants rolled up (shoulders slumped, eyes down)—there isn't a single shadow anywhere on the beach (the smell of the salt residue is particularly seductive)—, swinging his frame, and sits down at the far end, a long way from the commotion.

He smokes facing the sea, thinking that there's nothing to keep him here—and there and then, sitting on the sand he wonders why (for what?). His life is passing with incredible, Tarkovskyan slowness, and all his old dreams have faded with the relentless competition of reality. If at least he was happy in his work—but he doesn't even have that: He's a minor bureaucrat, having to tolerate bosses infinitely more second-rate than he is, he thinks. It isn't even a matter of material comfort: His needs are few: He'd live more or less the same way in any part of the globe. It's all about the shock between reality and him: The inertia that stops him from breaking free of his stagnation; the false dilemma that ties him to nothingness.

The heat is criminal—it melts neurons, incites to violence, multiplies fertility tenfold. There isn't a beer for miles around (or water, or a barley drink, or anything that can be bought with the national currency). Nothing belongs to me, he thinks. And what about me, do I belong to anything? (The scratched record plays insistently.) All at once a group of young people appear carrying a strange object halfway between a ready-made and a broken wardrobe (there are six or seven carrying it); they pull the artifact to the water and get on it. The spectacle attracts a crowd of onlookers.

"Where are you going?"

"We're getting the fuck out of here."

"Nonstop to the USA."

"Have a good trip, guys."

"Take me with you, pal, don't be mean!"

By some miracle, the contraption floats; With a cry of Eureka, they set out to sea, rowing with broomsticks. Everything is crude (the raft, the oars, the crew, the country). The onlookers make a tremendous racket (some smile, others look worried) and he ends up going closer too, with a mixture of anxiety and envy. He's surprised there are no accusations—*gusanos!* traitors!—or other similar insults; on the contrary: The people appear to be part of the odyssey (the enthusiasm is contagious). The waves rock the boat, caressing what should be the keel, and six or seven faces laugh like kids with a new toy: They won't make it, he thinks, seeing the raft move away and disappear amid the waves.

19

For an hour, the onlookers stay in the same place, talking among themselves, recounting what they've seen to other people who approach (flies, he thinks, surrounding the scratched record of shit). He chose this spot thinking it would be quiet and now he's seen himself overtaken by reality. There have always been crazy people who throw themselves in the sea in unbelievable rafts; The unbelievable thing now is that it happens in broad daylight. He asks himself if he's been too immersed in his own thoughts to the point of not seeing what's happening around him, or if things are happening too quickly and he, wrapped up in his metaphysical crap, is unable to keep a grasp on events. It's as if his memory has also been subordinated to the great scratched record that governs life: Selective memory, rabbit-

like memory, clear memory, correct and fil-
tered of impurities.

He heads back home. He enters the
apartment, takes off his shirt (he puts on a
Mussorgsky cassette), and calls the office,
inventing an excuse. The manager reassures
him.

"It's all right, son, but make sure you go
to the doctor"—he's never missed work
(even though he hates it) so his absence is a
cause for concern: "Are you sure you aren't
sick?"

"No, comrade, it's just . . . a little dis-
comfort."

He hangs up: Rum, cigarette, couch. He
picks up a book at random, opens it to any
old page, any old paragraph, any old line, and
reads from there, without paying attention.

The scratched record of daily life super-
imposes itself onto the story and, of course,
onto any hallucination about the future (the
only thing that really matters is today): The
rest is mental masturbation. He shuts himself in the bathroom with the Russian
woman in his head (taking advantage of the

fact that there's water, he takes an unhurried shower): He ejaculates, spattering the walls (he goes weak in the knees). He dries his body with an old, frayed towel; then he defecates: He's already a new man.

20

He wakes with a ray of sunlight tormenting his left eye, the hum of the fan settled in both eardrums, and the stickiness of summer soaking the sheets and the pillow. Without thinking, he calls a doctor friend and asks for a medical note (they agree to meet in a park they know from their childhood); he takes his camera, a few rolls of old film, and goes out. He walks along the seawall all the way to the end (he crosses through the tunnel on Fifth) and sits down to wait. To wait for what? For the scratched record of the inevitable to play out.

An hour later, a group of teenagers approaches the shoreline with planks, ropes, and empty barrels. In just under forty minutes, they put together a floating contraption of limited dimensions (they make a mast out of a pipe, and a sail from a number of sheets). A few gallons of water and cans of cookies will serve as sustenance for the crew. The kids prepare the raft—he photographs the process—until one of them (no older than seventeen) approaches and, with all the insolence of the barrio, asks him, "Man, you a cop or something?"

"No, no, no, me a cop? Forget it."

"It's like, I see you taking pictures, man."

"I'm just a witness of my time . . . "

The teenager looks at him as you would look at a misunderstood poet. "You're a fucking stoolie, that's what you are," and he turns, leaving him standing there, camera in hand, and no time to tell him to go fuck himself.

21

He's finishing the first rolls when the floating artifact sets off with its cargo of kids who are sick of it all and don't have anything to hold them back. While the raft heads for the straits, he sets off for home (dragging his feet) wondering at what moment the dream of the future got stuck in the past: Everything it was assumed we had left behind—he thinks—returns again (all the vices of the old regime, but today) like a screw that's lost its thread, or a record that gets scratched and turns around and around in the same place.

Everything is violence, he thinks: People are always on edge and any excuse, however minor it is, is enough to trigger crime. Hunger feeds us, despair is the one hope, he thinks. He gets to the park (across from a theater) where he meets his old friend.

Sitting on the rim of the waterless fountain, the doctor hands him the paper that makes him officially sick, freeing him from work for a few days. They both smoke and watch the children pass and remember the days when they too were children and played at being agents of the security forces

"I'm going," the doctor announces. "It's all over."

"I know," he replies. "I know . . . "

They part with a hug, knowing it will be the last, the final goodbye. He gets home and throws himself on the couch, tired, with no desire to think. He feels old, skinny, dirty, lost—what has changed since yesterday? He asks himself again if he's nothing more than a tortured aesthete, and he doesn't know what to reply. On one hand, like any other person in this scratched record he lives immersed in the epic of poor but dignified dignity, sacrifice as a modus vivendi, survival as self-improvement; on the other hand—he tortures himself—he doesn't understand why poverty is a work of art, or the highest stage of social evolution.

The twilight is slow, a hot micro-inferno in the middle of summer: A lethargy as big as the sea takes possession of life. He dozes off, letting himself be carried by images filled with sharks and corpses; he dreams that he bets on the eight (the dead man) and the ten (the big fish), winning a journey to the other world. He wakes bathed in sweat. It's nine o'clock, he knows that because of the thousands of TV sets around him all tuned in to the soap opera at high volume (the city comes to a standstill at that hour, hanging on other people's love affairs and dramas). He drags himself to the bathroom and throws a bit of water on himself, as an ineffectual solution to the heat. Then he makes a light, cold meal and devotes his night to a science-fiction movie. He sleeps on the couch, with the TV on, the balcony door open, and the minimal summer breeze sweetening his long sleep.

He wakes at six-thirty. He makes a strong cup of coffee without sugar and drinks it on the balcony, looking at the sea. He goes down to the bakery, where the people are standing and grumbling as they wait for their daily ration. He gets back to the apartment an hour later, knowing he's one of the privileged, that he doesn't depend, like others, only on his salary and the ration book: With the dollars his mother sends, he can stretch to a few luxuries—butter, yogurt, milk—allowing him to eat in a way that's unthinkable for many of his neighbors.

He devours his breakfast and smokes his first cigarette of the day with the news station on in the background. He reads a Russian novel. He's in a very good mood, he's slept well (in spite of the terrible state of the couch) and has several free days that he can add to his vacation. The news says nothing new (nothing he didn't hear yesterday, or last week, or the previous month) and he gradually stops paying attention to the monotony of the presenters. The novel, on the other hand, grabs him on each page, sinking into the announced tragedy of an anonymous, everyday person—so far, so alien, that he ends up feeling close to him.

Toward noon, he makes a frugal lunch and without stopping reading devours it in a few minutes. He's washing the plate and the frying pan when he hears voices in the corridor—first he takes no notice, thinking that it's a private matter, then, gradually, he understands that it's something less usual. New voices are added, questions are asked on all sides, there are concrete assertions (he hears the expression "Many died," and now there can be no doubt).

"What's going on?" he asks, going out into the corridor, where a group of five or six people are talking without stopping.

"My nephew who works in the harbor," a woman in her eighties starts saying, "called me just now: some individuals stole a boat."

"A boat?" he asks, surprised.

"Yes, yes, a boat, one of those they use in the harbor"—a tugboat, someone specifies. "They hijacked it to leave the country, and apparently it sank as it left the harbor."

"They sank it!" exclaims a neighbor, known for his eccentric opinions.

"How could they sink it? It sank!" replies a comrade, looking the eccentric in the eyes (a loud sarcastic burst of laughter can be heard).

"But when was this?"

"Last night, in the early hours, I don't know."

"I've been listening to the radio all morning and they didn't say anything."

"What could they have said, if they sank it themselves?" insists the eccentric (the comrade glares at him).

"And did anyone die?" he asks.

"Lots of them, apparently, but my nephew doesn't know how many. He says when he finds out more he'll call me back."

"It must be the work of the enemy!" the comrade cries with patriotic fervor.

"Of course! If the enemy's at home!"

The debate freezes when another neighbor appears with a uniform from head to feet (serious face, pistol at his belt) and quickly walks past the group.

"So, is it true?" they ask him.

"All I know is what they told me over the phone: that something very serious happened and I have to go to my unit as soon as possible"—he pauses—"but I don't like it," he says, before being swallowed up by the stairs.

He goes back to his apartment, just long enough to put his shoes on, change the roll in the camera, and go out to the street, where the sun strikes him as even more scorching than usual. He walks in the direction of the bay, observing attentively—pretending to be distracted—the huddles forming on the corners, among the people standing in line, and on the seawall. To all appearances, the scratched record of everyday life continues intact, repeating itself as it does every day; but deep down, something is moving, falling apart, breaking up.

He reaches the oldest part of the city and enters the harbor. There are lots of guards (public adornment): He can't get closer. A cop stands in his way and with regal courtesy advises him to beat it, comrade. He takes a few photographs. A small group is gesticulating, pointing to the old fort and then out to sea—he approaches—one of the guys asserts: "Yes, pal, I was standing right here last night, making out with my girl, and I saw it all, friend."

24

He stops outside the eighty-year-old woman's door, a little hesitant. Before he can ring the bell, she opens, always on the alert for any movement in the corridor (local chatter, no doubt unfairly, brands her a gossip).

"Er . . . I'd like to know if you have news from your nephew . . . You know, about what happened in the harbor."

The woman looks around, as if this is a bad spy movie, and murmurs conspiratorially:

"It's better to talk inside."

The apartment is a museum of useless objects: Russian dolls, images of saints, and Chinese ornaments of little aesthetic value, he thinks. He sits down on a red couch covered in transparent nylon and full of cushions and plastic dolls. The kitchen is from the Fifties: the refrigerator and the shelves, all Formica and enamel, with rounded corners and alarming proportions in the context of that small space. The woman pours some herbal tea into cups that look like porcelain (are they?), and starts her babble:

"My nephew says it wasn't an accident at all"—he raises an eyebrow—"he says there were orders from above to prevent that boat getting away"—he feigns surprise—"that first they hosed down the deck with water cannon—like firefighters," she adds, "and then they started to ram the boat until it sank."

"It sank?" he asks.

"Well, actually, the boys had orders to stop it, not sink it"—and the woman, with a startlingly coquettish gesture, winks at him with one eye while staring at him fixedly with the other. "There were about seventy of them, and at least thirty drowned."

Back in his apartment, he tunes to the news station to see if they say anything. He knows it's always like this; faced with a lack of information, all that is left is speculation and gossip. News items travel from mouth to mouth, getting distorted on the way (like a damned scratched record) until they become urban myths of more than dubious veracity. They spread like a virus in this defenseless organism, making any distinction between reality and fantasy, metafiction and fiction, impossible. There's a lack of verifiable sources, he thinks: Like the news, as unlikely as it is uncertain (next year production will increase by such and such percent; the new trade deal with China will raise our consumption capacity by this much percent, the radio headlines recite). He eats rice and fried eggs without any appetite, all the while asking himself what's going to happen now. He goes blank for a few minutes, staring engrossed at the wall. The question returns, obsessively, and the wall doesn't answer.

25

He goes up to see the Russian woman. He knows that she receives foreign radio every day: That's how he finds her, sitting by the radio. The scratched record of criticism from overseas echoes around the living room of her small apartment, as square and Soviet as the building. The Russian woman bites her lip, anxiously. Political nature has operated in her since childhood: When she was little, she received letters from her parents, both guests in Siberia, and at one time in her life she herself was accused of the worst crime of all: doing business.

They sent her to this inhospitable island, a last chance to go to the heaven of the righteous: She came to redeem herself and ended up black marketeering, he thinks. He observes her on the sly (her hard, stiff beauty, and that warm smile of hers). He thinks he's starting to fall in love with her, and is surprised: He comes to the conclusion that she is the only thing dear to him in his life. She asks:

"You're going too, aren't you?"

They look at each other for minutes, maybe years, and he doesn't answer. They converse in silence, accompanied by the muffled noises of the city and a pathetic bolero spewing out apathetically from the radio.

26

He calls a former classmate from the university, whose interest in the mechanics of cameras led him to become passionate about photography itself. He goes to visit him just after the soap opera, with a bottle of rum, some cigarettes, and two undeveloped rolls.

The kitchen is transformed into a small darkroom; on the little table there appear a Czech enlarger and trays of developer, fixer, and water, and they spend the next hour developing and printing a few copies.

"Things are getting bad," his friend says with cinematic gravity. "This is a shipwreck and the rats are abandoning the ship. Mark my words: The revolution has failed," he says, not devoid of grandiloquence and provocation (enfant terrible), he thinks. He used to be truly fat, Pavarottian, with a spirit the size of the universe; now he's skinny and dull, lacking in charisma. Anemia has stripped him of his identity. His optimism disappeared along with his belly, as if that had been the precise measure of his hopes and happiness.

"It isn't just failing," he continues, "but it insists on dragging us down with it. And what the fuck can we do? Do you realize we've always been part of this? What are we going to do now?" cries the former fat man, on his third or fourth rum.

He lights a cigarette, smiles faintly like an old, badly paid clown, and starts to sum up:

"First, this island is sinking into the sea—"

"That's the problem," the former fat man cuts in, "the island is sinking and we can't blame anyone else. We've torpedoed ourselves. Mark my words: ourselves."

"Of course," he intervenes as if the thing were of little importance. "Do you know anything about the tugboat they sank?"

"What tugboat?" the former fat man

retorts. "Boy, haven't you learned that things only happen if the news says they happen? Have you heard an official version?" At his negative gesture, the former fat man continues, "If they haven't said anything, it means nothing happened. And that isn't up for debate, comrade."

They drink rum for hours. The alcohol invites inevitable nostalgia, that scratched record of the distant past . . .

"What about my photographs?" he asks. "What do you think?"

"Boy," the former fat man replies, "for a beginner they aren't bad. What camera do you use?"

"A Kiev," he replies.

The former fat man looks at him sarcastically. "Pal, that's not a camera, it's a device that's useless for contemporary photographic practice."

"What?"

"Throw that shit in the garbage, man, it's no good for anything." The former fat man goes to a cupboard filled with parts and cameras and comes back with a black

Pentax (old, solid), two lenses (a 35 and a 200), and a flash. "This is a basic but decent kit. It's a loan," he adds. "The only thing I ask is that you take good photographs. This won't last: We're making history, comrade."

They part and he starts to head home. He traverses the night, bumping into things, bouncing between walls and doubts. We aren't making history, he thinks: We're being carried away by it. Like the currents of the sea. We're getting farther and farther from the coast. We're drifting: History is sweeping us along. After decades of trying to tame it, it's rebelled. We haven't been able to transform it, and now we have to pay the price.

A day is scratched . . .

27

They're knocking angrily at the door. His hangover has him frozen. He was sleeping with his clothes on, including shoes, and now with more than questionable balance he gets up. The eighty-year-old woman's smile fades when she sees him, although she is too polite to make a vulgar or inappropriate comment.

She shows him the newspaper:

"You see? I told you there'd been an accident," she says, pointing to a paragraph. "An irresponsible act of piracy . . . an unfortunate accident."

"Good," he murmurs. "That means we can have a clear conscience."

The woman smiles. "Conscience maybe. All the rest is worry," and she goes, closing the door delicately.

The office manager on the telephone:

"Listen . . . I know you're sick but you have to be there this afternoon; there's going to be an emergency meeting. I assume you've read today's paper."

"Yes, I have, comrade, a neighbor brought it to me. The truth is that ever since I heard the rumor I've been keeping up to date with the news."

"Very good," he can almost imagine the manager slapping him on the shoulder condescendingly, "as I'm sure you'll understand, we cannot permit a few traitors, drug addicts, and criminals to get away with it. We have to do something. And something drastic . . . "

"Of course, comrade. The nation comes first," and he hangs up.

The nation as otherness, which demands the death of those who comprise it, he thinks. An institution surrounded by enemies, always paranoid, calls to us. We owe it everything. Our first obligation is to it. Without it we are nothing, he thinks.

He takes some coffee and an aspirin, then a tortilla. On the radio they talk about what happened, and he intuits that this type of event will give rise to other similar ones. It happened with the Mariel boatlift, he thinks (the fire spread though the country as if it were a dry cane field). It's three-thirty when he leaves for the office, cutting through the rarefied atmosphere of the city. The buses and cars advance by inertia, people are falling asleep, the buildings are melting in a Daliesque manner: tropical surrealism.

The meeting is presided over by a skinny young guy (well-trimmed mustache, 26th of July sweater, blue jeans) who explains in a rabble-rouser's voice why we have to be alert and prevent (he emphasizes the word) any occurrence outside the established norms.

"Prevent how?" someone asks loudly.

"By force if necessary!" screams the orator, who is on the verge of either hysteria or ecstasy. "Yes, comrades! By force if necessary!"

At that moment, without knowing why, he raises his hand, gets to his feet and in a slow, deliberate voice states:

"I'm not going to suppress anybody," and a tragic silence falls. Dozens of faces turn toward him (the scene unfolds in slow motion, with not much depth of field), mouths open.

"What are you saying?" asks the orator with a mixture of surprise and indignation, not very accustomed to having people say no to him.

"I'm saying I'm not going to suppress anybody," he replies firmly; and without adding anything more he takes his party card from his pocket, goes to the table, and drops the card on it, without heroism, as if it was the most natural, most obvious thing in the world, the only thing possible in the present circumstances. "I'm not going to suppress anybody."

And he turns and goes.

30

He's tired. His world is collapsing: He receives summonses, they're investigating him, delving into his life. He's lost his job, of course, and is left with his meager savings and some of the money his mother sends. With this stain on his record, there's already nothing to be done: He knows he's fucked. On the balcony, in his shorts, he follows the events as if they had nothing to do with him—he observes, calculates. He dresses in light clothes and goes out toward the seawall. He carries his camera slung over his shoulder.

Everything begins suddenly. He photographs a group gathered on a corner. Then others approach, and still others, and in an instant, as if it's a piece of theater—a performance, a happening—they all start to cry *down with* and *death to*! (It seems like the end of the world, or at least its announcement.) And so it continues. For the first time in his life, he witnesses the beautiful sight of a spontaneous demonstration, not the scratched record of a staged event. To be witness to a genuine, albeit minimal, revolt makes him, for a split second, regain his optimism.

Windows are smashed, metal rods come out. A mob from some brigade or other appears on a corner to crush the rebels: There's a pitched (medieval) battle: one horde against another, pipes and stones as ammunition—war cries, opened skulls, lost eyes, lost lives . . . The unthinkable is becoming reality, even if only for a moment. Hours later, the leader appears in his jeep, surrounded by his people. The streets fill with the faithful, who must have been hiding. *Vivas!* sound. The fire is going out . . .

31

For weeks, he wanders with his camera along the city's coasts, photographing the world that is escaping—faces smile at the adventure of escape, the adolescent provocation of running away from home. He witnesses with surprise the uncommon spectacle of police officers watching without intervening (there are no blows, no arrests, they just watch from a distance). At the seawall, groups form to encourage those who leave (applause, good luck wishes, cries of support): a collective party, a mass farewell, a joyful service. A liturgy. He never thought that the scratched record of daily life could sound like that, that the city could be transformed to that extent. It's not that society is disintegrating, it's that right now there is no social body (we are predators, he thinks: trying to devour our fellow man). Hunger unites us, yes, but also make us prey for the strongest—and always, he thinks, there is someone stronger than ourselves.

Every day they hear news (or gossip, how can they know?) of those who make it and those who don't. Whole families disappear into the sea—statistics, a topic of conversation. Weeks and weeks watching the city empty out; not a day goes by that he doesn't hear about some friend or acquaintance who has left (the doctor, the former fat man, his ex-wife, so many others): The nine o'clock soap opera is replaced by the soap opera of daily life. The scratched record of politics is repeated again and again: Workers can be sacrificed, the straits are the notice board: We are dispensable, trash tossed into the sea, he thinks.

32

A noise—a crackle—and the cycle starts again. He can't sleep: The hour is getting closer. The storm pounds the coast, the waves rise against the wall, the wind howls like a broken bassoon, and the natural darkness coincides with the scheduled power outage. He settles down in the kitchen with half a bottle, by the light of a candle (a black stain runs through the barrio, fusing with the sea). The hours don't pass—time comes to a halt. The voices of the citizens cannot be heard. He takes his backpack (full of negatives and undeveloped rolls), puts on a raincoat, and covers the camera with a plastic bag. He goes out. He meets the others as they prepare the raft, they arrange the final details. It's a wooden hulk some fifteen feet by six, with gasoline tanks as floats and an outboard motor from a Russian washing machine: Only we could call this shit a raft, he thinks. They load the provisions (water, hard bread, preserves stolen from God knows where), the gear (a compass, toy binoculars, a flare that nobody's sure will work, fishing line, and bait), and talk without stopping. He records the process in the merciless rain. He lives it as a photo story (his own: the one that'll make him famous when he gets there, his farewell to anonymity and mediocrity, his true profession, he thinks). Everything is ready. They throw themselves in. The sea seems infinite . . .

Day breaks as the raft moves off, lurching over the swell (in the rain, struck by the wind, subject to the ups and downs of chance). For the first time in his life, he sees the city from the sea and thinks it looks like a worn-down old whore who hasn't completely lost her beauty. He also thinks he's going to miss her.

At about ten, they encounter the coast guard. The launch approaches and they are asked if they have what they need (the dozen or so photographers, film cameramen, and journalists who are with the coast guard insist on interviewing them, even though they have to yell). He, in his turn, photographs the coast guard. They tell them the cyclone will hit them in the straits, that it's better if they turn back and try again in a few days.

"No way! We're going!"

Dizzy, he agrees with the coast guard. He knows, nevertheless, that there's no turning back: The die is cast.

By four, the sea looks like a chain of black mountains and snow-covered peaks; the sky is a negative of itself, the sun has stopped existing, and everyone starts to suspect that indeed the cyclone has arrived. The swell has detached one of the drums that have been keeping them afloat, and the raft, limping, does what it can to continue its wandering. They blame each other, the disaster is coming closer—one weeps, another prays, someone laughs hysterically, and so on, going through all the stages of understanding the failure. He, in a corner, calmly photographs the scene. He wants to smoke, but by now the cigarettes have turned into a foul-smelling paste, devoid of identity. The camera is soaked; he suspects that these photographs will never be developed.

They climb a mile-high wave; from the top they see the mouth of the abyss. For a few eternal seconds, they contemplate the teeth of the sea (the throat of Neptune, the snout of the end) and begin the descent, aware that it's all over. Another wave hits them from the side: The boat lurches and falls apart.

Reaching the eddy, they sink, turning like a scratched record.

At thirty-three revolutions per minute . . .